Invitations to Personal Reading
Curriculum Foundation Classroom Library
Scott, Foresman and Company

Books to Read Aloud

The Big Golden Book of Poetry	edited by Jane Werner
Finders Keepers	Will and Nicolas
Little Frightened Tiger	Golden MacDonald
The Man Who Didn't Wash His Dishes	Phyllis Krasilovsky
The Old Woman and Her Pig	illustrated by Paul Galdone
Rosa-Too-Little	Sue Felt
Six Foolish Fishermen	retold by Benjamin Elkin
The Three Billy Goats Gruff	P. C. Asbjørnsen and J. E. Moe
Umbrella	Taro Yashima
Where Does the Butterfly Go When It Rains	May Garelick

Books to Enrich the Content Fields

The Big Book of Real Fire Engines	illustrated by George Zaffo
The Listening Walk	Paul Showers
One Snail and Me	Emilie McLeod
The Sky Was Blue	Charlotte Zolotow
What Is A Turtle	Gene Darby

Books for Independent Reading

Belling the Cat and Other Stories	retold by Leland Jacobs
Big Talk	Miriam Schlein
Cowboy Small	Lois Lenski
Gertie the Duck	Nicholas Georgiady and Louis Romano
Indian Two Feet and His Horse	Margaret Friskey
Josie and the Snow	Helen Buckley
Karen's Opposites	A. and M. Provensen
Millions and Millions and Millions!	Louis Slobodkin
Nothing but Cats, Cats, Cats	Grace Skaar
Robins and Rabbits	John Hawkinson

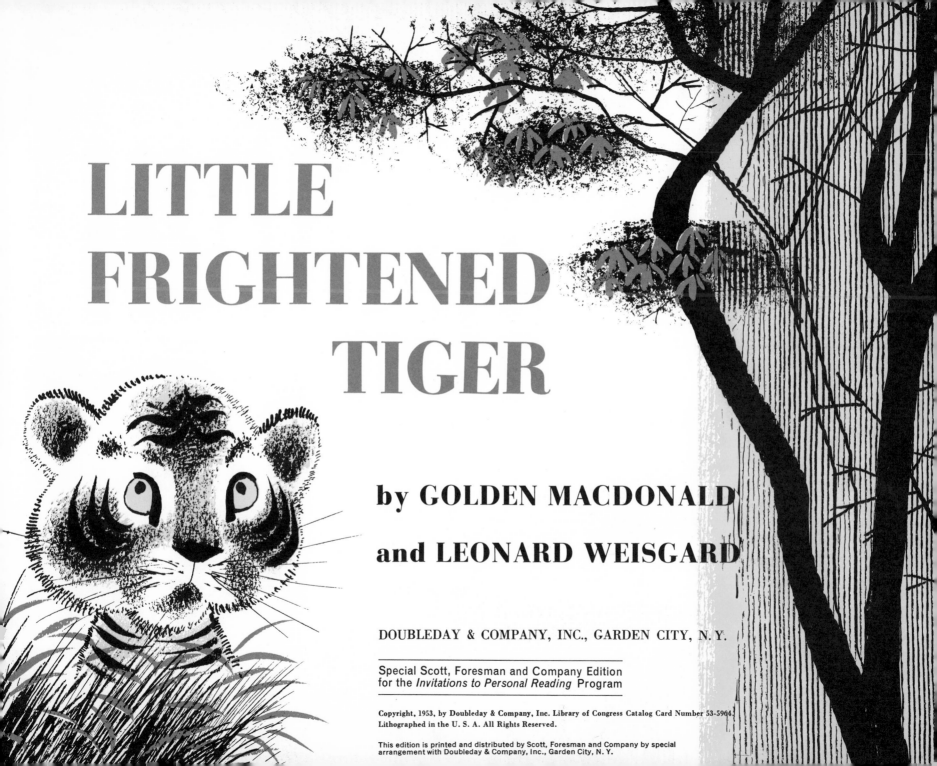

LITTLE FRIGHTENED TIGER

by GOLDEN MACDONALD
and LEONARD WEISGARD

DOUBLEDAY & COMPANY, INC., GARDEN CITY, N. Y.

Special Scott, Foresman and Company Edition
for the *Invitations to Personal Reading* Program

This edition is printed and distributed by Scott, Foresman and Company by special
arrangement with Doubleday & Company, Inc., Garden City, N. Y.

Once there was a little tiger who was absolutely scared to death. He shook in the morning. He shook in the bright hot sun at noon. He shook in the sunset when the golden shadows fell with their last long rays on the tawny backs of the tigers who had all come out on the warm rocks. And he shook all night, and he woke up in the morning shaking. He was scared to death, the poor little tiger.

His mother and father, who were tigers, were very, very brave tigers, as all tigers are brave — "brave as a lion, fierce as a tiger, fierce as a lion, brave as a tiger." That is the way it was. But at any rate, this little tiger was a frightened tiger. And so one day his mother said: "Little tiger, stop shaking or you will shake your little stripes off."

And the little tiger said, "But I am frightened and I am afraid." And they said, "Well, don't be afraid, little tiger, because everybody is afraid of something, but tigers never show it."

"And what are you afraid of?"

"I don't know," said the little tiger. "I am afraid of the sun and the wind and the rain. I am afraid of tigers and rabbits and mice.

"I just am a frightened little tiger."

"Well," said his mother and father, "don't be afraid, little tiger. Come with us and walk right between us."

"Where will we go?" said the little tiger. "I am afraid to go anywhere."

"Don't be afraid with us," said his mother and father. "Your mother will walk on your right side and your father will walk on your left side and we will walk around our world. And we will show you in all parts of this world how everybody is afraid of something."

So the tigers walked through the jungle. And as they walked through the jungle where they lived, all the other animals ran away, because everyone in the jungle was afraid of the tigers.

"Do you see that?" said his mother.

"I do indeed," said the little tiger.

And as he reached the edge of the jungle he stopped shaking.

And they walked on to the great grassy plains where the great, gray, grave and gigantic elephants grazed. The elephants were not afraid of tigers. "Elephants are not afraid of anything. They are so big." Or at least it seemed as though the elephants were not afraid of anything.

Until along came a little mouse out of a hole in the grass.

Now, elephants are afraid of a mouse.

And when the elephants, the great grave and gargantuan elephants, saw this little tiny gray mouse, they trumpeted to the skies, and switched their little elephant tails across their great gray, vast and gargantuan bottoms, and galloped off, and lumbered off, and tumbled away across the plains.

"Ha-ha," said the little tiger.

"Did you see that?" said his mother.

"Did you see that?" said his father.

"I did indeed," said the little tiger.

"Elephants are afraid of a mouse."

And by the time they reached the edge of the great grassy plains the little tiger wasn't so frightened and he was not afraid.

"What's a mouse afraid of?" he asked suddenly.

"A mouse is afraid of his own shadow," whispered the father just as the sun went down.

And, sure enough, there was a little mouse running for all he was worth with his shadow right behind him.

The little tiger chuckled. "So a mouse is afraid of his own shadow?" he said.

"Indeed he is," said his mother.

"Indeed he is," said his father.

And, as the sun went down this little tiger was not afraid.

They walked all that night through the bright moonlight. And up in the tree tops the monkeys were chattering away.

"What are monkeys afraid of?" asked the little tiger.

"Monkeys are afraid of airplanes," said his mother.

And just then, through the moonlight, slowly, like a giant moth whose wings were still, a great airplane flew through the night. And all the monkeys chattered and screamed and whistled in the tree tops and dove into hollow trees and hung by their tails like bunches of bananas as they huddled together.

"Ha-ha," said the little tiger. "So monkeys are afraid of airplanes."

"Indeed they are," said his mother.

"Indeed they are," said his father.

"Indeed they are," said the little tiger. And he walked bravely through the moonlight under the monkey trees, and he wasn't afraid, all night.

And he walked along and sang a tiger's brave little song:

"I am a brave little tiger, ho-ho, ho-ho.

I am not frightened wherever I go go go.

My mother and father walk by my side

And I am a little tiger, inside."

He could not think of any more song because just then the sun came up and he started to shake.

"Don't be frightened," said his mother, as the sun rose over the great green sea and a fish jumped out of the water.

"What's that?" said the little tiger, shaking all over.

"That," said his mother, "is a fish."

"And what are fish frightened of?" said the little tiger.

"Fish are frightened of ships. And other fish. And bigger fish," said his father.

Just then along came swimming a whale and right behind the whale came a ship — a whaling ship. And the whale swam like thunder through the water and dove down to the bottom of the ocean just as the ship sailed by.

"Ho-ho," said the little tiger, "even a whale is afraid of something."

"Indeed he is," said the little tiger's mother.

"Indeed he is," growled the tiger father.

Then the tigers walked away from the ocean and crossed the river. And as the sun came up at high noon and the tigers lay on the shore, basking their fur in the warm downright rays of the great round sun, the little tiger began to shiver.

Now, his mother lay on one side of him and his father lay on the other side of him, and they said, "Don't be afraid, little tiger. What is there that frightens you at high noon?"

Just then a little bird flew over, flying for all his might, and the little tiger nearly jumped out of his stripes.

"Quiet, quiet, my little tiger," said his mother. "Surely you are not afraid of a little bird? I never heard of a tiger who was afraid of a bird."

"What are little birds afraid of?" asked the little tiger.

"Little birds are afraid of bigger birds."

And just then a great hawk sailed slowly through the sky.

"Ha-ha," said the little tiger. "So little birds are afraid of hawks."

"Yes," said his father, "indeed they are."

They walked on and on. And toward sundown they came to a turn in the river. Big white two-footed creatures with long legs, long necks and big toenails on big sharp pointed feet stalked up and down at the water's edge.

"What's that?" said the little tiger, shaking from head to toe.

"Those are storks," said his father.

"I am afraid," said the little tiger.

"Don't be afraid of storks," laughed his mother.

"What are they afraid of," asked the little tiger.

"Babies," said his mother, "any kind of baby. Watch them.

They jump when babies flap at them.

They squawk when babies snap at them.

And when babies cry they fly up in the air all at once."

The little tiger was still shivering.

"But don't be afraid," said his mother and father.

"Storks are even scared of baby tigers," said the father.

"So they are," said the little tiger. The storks flapped away into

the air when the little tiger walked down to the river bank.

And so they were. Afraid of a baby tiger!

"Let's go home," yawned the little tiger just as the sun went down. "Let's go home as fast as we can."

So the tigers walked away as the sun set under the clouds like a glorious streak of lightning. And the next thing they knew, they were back in their own dear jungle, where the little tiger never shook again and was not afraid of anything, except himself.

"**I** am a brave little tiger, ho-ho, ho-ho.

I am not frightened wherever I go go go.

My mother and father walk by my side

And I am a little tiger, inside."